Zoomi & Zoe
and the
Tricky Turnaround

Written by COREY ANN HAYDU
Illustrated by ANNE APPERT

QUIRK BOOKS
PHILADELPHIA

This is a work of fiction. All names, places, and characters are products of the author's imagination or are used fictitiously. Any resemblance to real people, places, or events is entirely coincidental.

Copyright © 2025 by Corey Ann Haydu
Illustrations copyright © 2025 by Anne Appert

All rights reserved. Except as authorized under U.S. copyright law, no part of this book may be reproduced in any form without written permission from the publisher.

Library of Congress Cataloging-in-Publication Data
Names: Haydu, Corey Ann, author. | Appert, Anne, illustrator.
Title: Zoomi and Zoe and the tricky turnaround / written by Corey Ann Haydu ; illustrated by Anne Appert.
Description: Philadelphia : Quirk Books, 2025. | Series: Zoomi and Zoe ; 1 | Audience term: Children | Audience: Ages 4–8 | Summary: Zoe and her stuffed rhino Zoomi learn to navigate change together when both their best friends move away.
Identifiers: LCCN 2024033227 (print) | LCCN 2024033228 (ebook) | ISBN 9781683694588 (hardcover) | ISBN 9781683694595 (ebook)
Subjects: CYAC: Adjustment–Fiction. | Friendship–Fiction. | Toys–Fiction.
Classification: LCC PZ7.H31389 Zo 2025 (print) | LCC PZ7.H31389 (ebook) | DDC [Fic]–dc23
LC record available at https://lccn.loc.gov/2024033227
LC ebook record available at https://lccn.loc.gov/2024033228

ISBN: 978-1-68369-458-8

Printed in China

Typeset in Lazy One and Proxima Sera

Designed by Andie Reid

Quirk Books
215 Church Street
Philadelphia, PA 19106
quirkbooks.com

10 9 8 7 6 5 4 3 2 1

To my sweet, sunny,
funny Thisbe
For being exactly you

Welcome to GlumbleGlibble!

Zoomi lives in GlumbleGlibble and resembles a rhino stuffie from the Human world. She is full of energy, doesn't like change, and absolutely loves to zoom.

Zoe lives in Sherborn, a small town in the Human world. She loves making lists, following rules, and having a best friend.

Izly

Zoomi   Zoe

Izly is a friend of Zoomi's who is always there to help, explain, and take charge.

Moo is Zoomi's very best friend, who is leaving GlumbleGlibble for a new home far away from Zoomi.

Doug is always Doug! A gentle mer-unicorn who is kind and careful and silly.

MOO   DOUG

Chapter One

There was one thing Zoomi loved: parties.

And there was one place Zoomi didn't want to be: Moo's party.

Not because Zoomi didn't like Moo. In fact, Zoomi loved Moo. Moo was Zoomi's best friend.

Which is exactly why Zoomi didn't want to be at his going away party.

There were starcakes and a cloud house

and dinosaur rides. But Zoomi would give up a hundred dinosaur rides if it meant Moo could stay.

"I can't stay," Moo said when Zoomi asked for the fifty-third time. They were eating starcakes while waiting for their turn to go down the rainbow mud slide. "We

have a new home now. Three hours away."

Zoomi didn't know much about hours, but three sounded like too many. And she could not think of anywhere better than Moo's cave, where he lived now. Except for maybe Doug's bubble palace. Or Izly's treetop home. Or Zoomi's own invisible castle. But Moo's parents had found some other cave in some other place, far away from Zoomi.

"Your turn," Moo said. He always let Zoomi go first.

Zoomi went splat onto her furry stomach and did a slip-slide-swoosh down the rainbow mud. When she got up, her fur had turned every color of the rainbow. Moo went down next. His slippery scales made him go extra fast. When he got to the bottom, his parents said it was time to go.

The party was over.

"Don't worry," Moo said when Zoomi started to cry. "This is our Tricky Turn-around! And you know what that means."

Zoomi was crying so hard she only heard the last word Moo said.

"It *is* mean!" she replied. "It is *so* mean that your parents are making you move away!"

Moo tried again.

"No, Zoomi, that's not what I said. I said it's our *Tricky Turnaround*. We'll finally get our Happy Helpful Humans! And they'll get us! And then you'll go down the rainbow mud slide together."

Zoomi wiped away some tears. How had she forgotten? Her Happy Helpful Human! She had been waiting her whole life for this!

"I'm really going to get one?" Zoomi asked.

"We both are," Moo said.

Zoomi swallowed. Moo's Human was the luckiest. Moo's Human got to have Moo. But first, Moo had to leave Zoomi. That was the sad part.

There couldn't be a Tricky Turnaround and a Happy Helpful Human without the sad part.

And the sad part was really, really sad.

That's what made it so tricky.

Chapter Two

Zoe's best friend Kyla had been gone for three hours, and they were already the worst three hours of Zoe's life. Zoe was sure about this, because Zoe had made a list of the worst hours in her life. Zoe made lists for most things.

Here was the list of what made these three hours the worst ones ever:

> Reasons these are the worst 3 hours
>
> 1. Dad burned the burgers for lunch
> 2. Can't find doll's purple shoes or Zoomi
> 3. Pretty sure I'm getting the sniffles

None of these things were *that* bad, but somehow burnt burgers and a sniffly nose were way worse without a best friend around. Everything was worse without Kyla. Zoe's room seemed darker. Her favorite stuffed rhino, Zoomi, was strangely missing. Maybe it was in a corner of Kyla's house, waiting for her to come back and get it. And now she never would.

Even though technically Zoomi was just a stuffie, Zoe was pretty sure Zoomi was very silly, with a loud laugh and a hundred excellent ideas and maybe even the ability to fly or bake the world's best cakes or something.

Now there was no Kyla *and* no Zoomi.

Plus, she was pretty sure her chair at the kitchen table had gotten wobblier.

"Can we visit Kyla tomorrow?" Zoe asked her dad.

"Oh, Zoe, she just left. We'll visit her soon. In a few months. Okay?"

It was *not* okay. A few months was *not* soon. A few months was forever.

"What about the day after tomorrow?" Zoe asked. She needed a plan. They needed to put it in the calendar in red pen like all their other most important plans.

Her dad chuckled, but it was not funny. Zoe stomped upstairs. She and Kyla had started making a collage of pink and green things, and Zoe tried to keep working on that. But her scissors weren't sharp enough and she couldn't find any green pictures in the magazine she was using, and when she tried to glue a pink rose onto the collage, the glue got everywhere.

Zoe liked neat collages. They should have decided exactly how much green and exactly how much pink and have a better system for applying glue.

Zoe liked systems almost as much as she liked lists and plans.

"UGHHHHHGRRRRRRRAGHHHHHH!" Zoe yelled.

She crumpled up the collage. As soon as it was in the trash can, she missed it.

"Quiet, sweetie, I'm trying to work!" called Papa, her other dad, which only made Zoe angrier. And sadder. And lonelier.

RRAGHHHHHH!

Chapter Three

"We need at least thirty-seven balloons and twelve pounds of confetti. *Glitter* confetti. And a cake. Chocolate. And vanilla. And then *another* layer of chocolate. With rainbow sprinkles. And frosting flowers."

Izly and Doug were taking notes as fast as they could, but it was not fast enough.

"We need to make a banner. A glitter banner. Really big. It should say *Welcome,*

Human! Does that sound weird? Maybe it should say, *I Already Love You So Much!* Because I do. Or maybe the banner should say *I Have Been Waiting My Whole Life to Meet You!* What do you think? I guess we should make all three to be safe?" She nodded to herself. "What else?"

Izly and Doug shrugged. They hadn't had their Tricky Turnarounds yet either, so they didn't know much about Happy Helpful Humans. They tried to remember what they knew about Humans in general.

"Humans brush their teeth!" Izly exclaimed. "So maybe we should have toothpaste?"

"Toothpaste! Yes. Lots of toothpaste," Zoomi agreed.

"Oh! Humans wear shoes!" Doug remembered.

"Shoes!" Zoomi was getting so excited she could hardly breathe. "We can make shoes, right? Maybe we should all wear shoes to greet my Human? Or we could make a shoe sculpture. So they know we respect that they like wearing shoes?"

"Shoe sculpture," Izly said. "Smart."

"And we'll need music. Humans like music," Zoomi said. "Something happy. And loud."

"A tuba?" Doug suggested.

"A tuba." Zoomi smiled. Perfect. Her Happy Helpful Human would feel so welcomed! She was sure of it. And of course, the day would end with the most important part of a Human's first day in GlumbleGlibble: holding hands down the rainbow mud slide.

Zoomi was nervous. She had never had a Human before, so she had never held hands with one going down the slide before. She hoped the slide would be slippy and slidey enough.

The friends got to work.

They made a chocolate-vanilla-chocolate

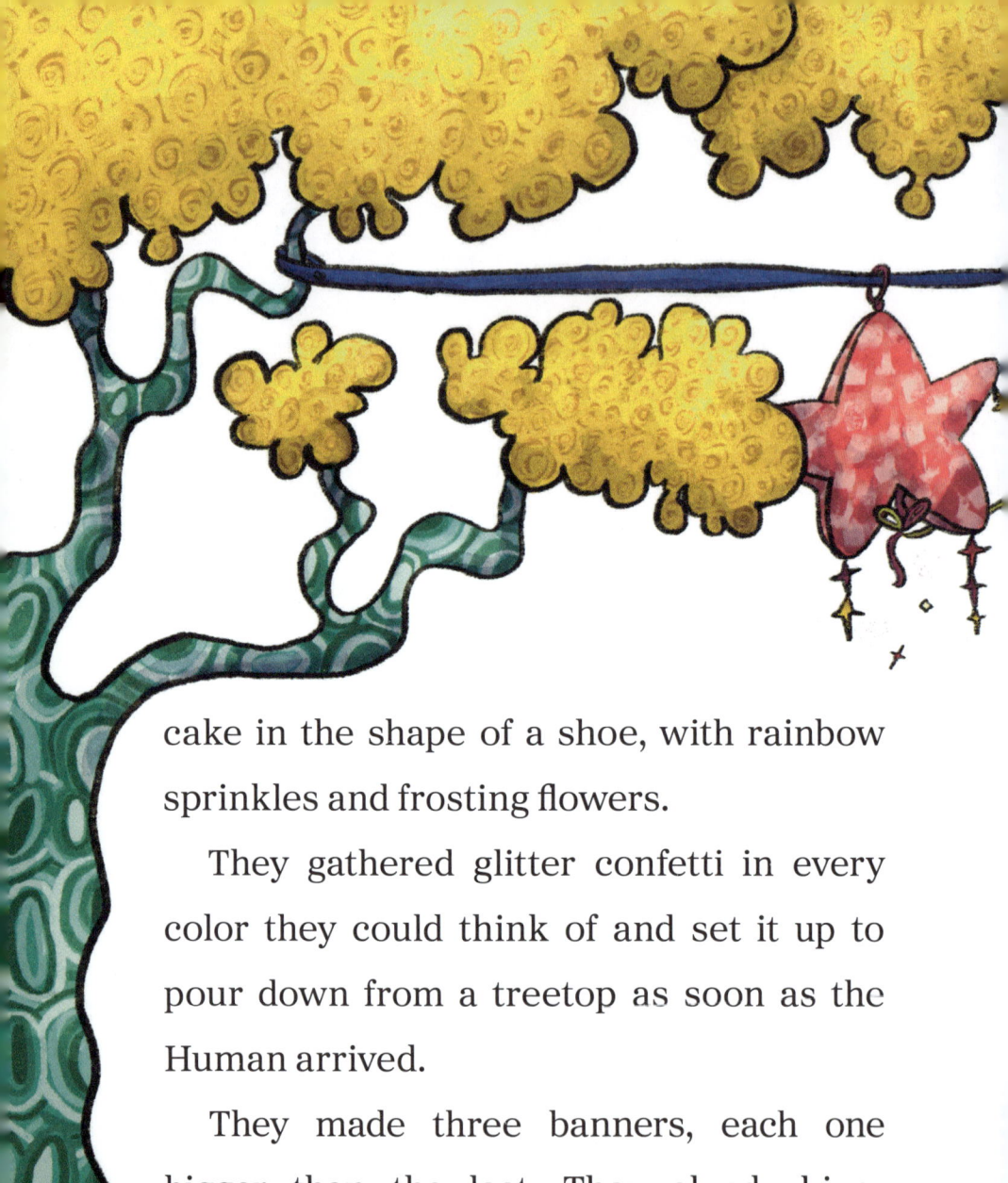

cake in the shape of a shoe, with rainbow sprinkles and frosting flowers.

They gathered glitter confetti in every color they could think of and set it up to pour down from a treetop as soon as the Human arrived.

They made three banners, each one bigger than the last. They glued rhinestones and pom-poms and toothbrushes

to the banners. They mixed up some extra rainbow mud for the slide.

And they made a pile of toothpaste so big that it was more of a mountain than a pile.

Zoomi just knew her Happy Helpful Human would love it.

Chapter Four

"Can we visit Kyla *now*?" Zoe asked Dad, after what was definitely a hundred and ten years.

"You asked me that five minutes ago," Dad said. He was less cheery this time.

"But I'm bored!" Zoe said. Zoe hated being bored even more than she hated cooked spinach or long car rides or writing a lowercase *q*.

"Then play outside," Dad said. Sometimes it seemed like Dad hated talking about being bored, even more than he hated having to change out of his favorite green sneakers and more than he hated when the sink in the bathroom wouldn't stop dripping.

Zoe knew there was nothing to do outside. But there was nothing to do inside either, so off she went. She lay on the grass. It smelled too grassy. She tried to look at the sky, but it was too sunny. So she closed her eyes. The air was too breezy and also too hot, which should have been impossible, but extra-awful things were possible when Kyla was gone.

She missed Kyla. She missed her rhino stuffie, Zoomi, who she still couldn't find and would probably never see again. She even missed the blue lizard stuffie Kyla had had since *she* was a baby. Its name was Moo. Probably Moo was sitting in the car next to Kyla, who was moving far, far away from Zoe.

Maybe Zoomi was far, far away, too.

Zoe was truly all alone. She closed her eyes and wished to be somewhere else. Somewhere better.

Chapter Five

"SHE'S HERE!" Doug screamed. Doug was the oldest and always the first to know everything, like what time the moon smiled each day, and how many creatures would go to the Creature Carnival every September. And today, Doug was the first to know that Zoomi's Happy Helpful Human had arrived.

"ZOOMI! *SHE'S HERE!*" Doug yelled again. Zoomi looked up and over the highest cloud mountain to the pineapple

portal that Humans walked through when they came to Happy Helpful Human Hill in GlumbleGlibble to help with someone's Tricky Turnaround.

And Doug was right. There she was.

A Happy Helpful Human.

She had one long braid and two green clips. She was wearing a tutu and a sweatshirt—and, just as Zoomi had predicted, shoes.

"GO!" Zoomi yelled. Izly and Doug sprang into action. Izly rolled out the cake and pulled the string that let out the confetti. Doug unfurled the banners and started playing the tuba.

Zoomi did what Zoomi did best, which was zoooooom toward her. Fast. Faster than fast.

"Human Human Human! You're here!" Zoomi stood up tall and smiled. She wanted to be sure her Human would recognize her. Humans were supposed to recognize their GlumbleGlibblers. Zoomi had been told they had toy versions of their GlumbleGlibblers in their Human world. Zoomi would like to see a toy version of herself! But of course the toy version of Zoomi was gone, now that they were meeting in real life. Surely her Human understood all of that already. It was pretty simple.

There was glitter everywhere. It got all over the Human's long braid and sweatshirt and tutu. "Look! We have toothpaste!" Zoomi said. "And the cake is shaped like a shoe!" Zoomi cut the Human a piece of cake and made sure to give her four frosting flowers. Zoomi danced along with the tuba music. She pulled the string again for more glitter to come down. "Are you ready to hold hands down the rainbow mud slide so that we can be best best best friends forever and ever and ever???"

But something was wrong.

The Human shrank to the ground and covered her head. "No more glitter, please! No more of that awful noise! Where am I? What's happening? What's a rainbow mud slide?"

This was not the greeting Zoomi wanted from her Human, who didn't seem very happy or even very helpful right now. Mostly her Human seemed scared.

"It's my Tricky Turnaround!" Zoomi explained. "I got you roller skates. And balloons!" Zoomi handed her Human shiny silver roller skates and fifty yellow balloons. She'd decided one hundred would be too many.

But maybe fifty was also too many, because the Human shrieked as the balloons floated up, up, up, and took her with them. Zoomi had forgotten that *her* balloons were bigger than Human balloons. A lot bigger. And a lot stronger.

Chapter Six

Some kind of talking bird flew right under Zoe and the balloons. "I've got her!" the bird-thing called.

"Put me down! Get me out of here!" Zoe cried.

"It's okay, I'll get you back down to the ground," the creature said. "My name is Izly. Don't worry, you're going to love the rainbow mud slide. I can tell."

"I want to go home!" Zoe said. She was crying even harder. "What is happening? Why am I here?"

"You're here to help Zoomi," Izly said, as if it was quite obvious. "You're a Happy Helpful Human."

"Who's Zoomi?" Zoe asked. The only Zoomi she'd ever known was her purple rhino stuffie.

"You know Zoomi!" Izly said. "Humans always recognize their GlumbleGlibbler. She's right there," Izly replied, pointing.

Zoe squinted, finally focusing on the very excited monster with purple and white and red and glittery fur, three golden horns, a red nose, and sparkly black eyes. She shook her head. Squinted some more. Izly set her on the ground.

Her purple rhino stuffie had not been glittery, and it had only one horn. And she had been the size of a normal stuffie, not the size of a terrifying monster. But she was the same shape, and she had the same eyes. The way she moved was the exact way she had always imagined her stuffie moving if she weren't, well, a stuffie. Zoe was sure of that.

"Zoomi is the one who gave me the balloons?" Zoe asked. "The rhino monster?"

"Well, that's rude," Izly said. "She's not a monster. Zoomi is just Zoomi. I'm just Izly. And Doug is obviously Doug."

"Oh," Zoe said. The tuba stopped playing. The bubble machine stopped bubbling.

"Sorry about the balloons," Zoomi said. "I just was so excited to meet you."

"Me? Why?" Zoe had so many questions, but she didn't know how to ask any of them.

"I've been waiting for you! What's your name? Humans have names, right?"

"Yes, we have—I'm Zoe," Zoe said.

"Zoe! Wow, how beautiful, I've never heard that before. Zoooooooe. Zo-oh-oh-oh-ee-ee-ee."

"I think there's been a mistake," Zoe said, interrupting Zoomi turning her name into a bouncy, tappy tune. "You were expecting me. But I don't know why I'm here."

"You're here to help me!" Zoomi said. "And I feel better already. My best friend, Moo, left town, but here you are, ready to fix it. What are you going to do first?"

Zoe shook her head. "I can't help you. I'm too sad to help anyone. My best friend moved away too," Zoe said. "Kyla. She moved to New Hampshire."

"Moo moved to the Forest of Aggle-Waggle-Loop-Di-Doo," Zoomi said.

"Oh."

They were both quiet for a while.

"Maybe we could help each other get our best friends back?" Zoe suggested. She

wasn't sure how that would work, but Zoomi did seem like she could do anything she set her mind to.

But Zoomi shook her head. "No, we're going to do something even better!"

Chapter Seven

"We have some important GlumbleGlibble business to do," Zoomi said. "But first we need to get everything ready. Vanish the tuba! Dump the glitter! Throw the cake far, far away! In fact, we should outlaw cake! Humans get very stressed out by cake and I hereby decree that GlumbleGlibble shall never have cake ever again!" Going down the rainbow mud slide with her Human was the most important thing that would ever happen, so everything needed to be perfect. And Zoomi was sure she could figure out how to make it exactly perfect for Zoe.

Doug twisted the tuba into a golden pretzel. Izly caught the glitter in a net. Zoomi picked up the beautiful cake and looked at her Happy Helpful Human.

Zoe's yellow sweatshirt had a shiny zipper on it. Her dark-blue backpack had its own, slightly less shiny zipper.

"Okay, let's turn the cake into a zipper!" Zoomi said. "Zoe loves zippers!" Zoomi put the cake down and lifted her hands into the air, about to magic the cake into the shiniest zipper that ever zipped. The cake wobbled and wiggled. But–

"Wait!" Zoe cried out. "Wait, I like cake!"

"No, you like zippers!" Zoomi said. "You have two zippers and no cakes. I should have known. I'm really good at some classes at school—like banana juggling and star singing and me-being—but I have never been very good at the study of Humans. But now I understand. You love shoes and toothpaste and zippers. Anything else? I know Humans have garbage cans in their homes, so you must love garbage? I'd rather not bring any here to GlumbleGlibble, but if you need it, I will."

Zoomi closed her eyes, ready to magic the cake into garbage instead, if that's what it took to make her Happy Helpful Human actually happy.

"No, we don't like garbage!" Zoe cried. "We don't even really care that much about zippers! But humans love cake! Or at least I do! And that one looks delicious! Please don't turn it into something else!"

"You're sure?" Zoomi asked.

"Positive," Zoe said. "Cake is my favorite food."

"Mine too!" Zoomi said. "We have so much in common! This is perfect, you can be my new best friend and stay here forever and ever and ever and never move away and eat lots of cake and you can teach me how to do zippers! Oh, I'm so relieved! Now let's eat cake and then we'll finally go to the rainbow mud slide so that we can be best friends and we'll make rainbow mud footprints all over GlumbleGlibble just like

Doug's sister's Human when they did it. Oh, it's going to be so fun and so funny and it's going to change everything forever!"

Zoomi cut Zoe the biggest piece of cake she could.

But still Zoe wasn't smiling.

"I can't stay forever," Zoe said. "Please don't make me."

Chapter Eight

"But we both miss our best friends and we both like cake more than garbage!" Zoomi said.

"That's, um, true, but I also like my home," Zoe said. "If I stayed, I'd miss my dads. And my bed."

"We have dads here!" Zoomi said. "And beds!" Zoomi crossed her arms.

Zoe wasn't sure what to say. She had never imagined arguing with a magical, real-life version of her favorite stuffed rhino. She would have to stay strong. This Zoomi was much more persuasive than the Zoomi at home, who was cuddly and droopy and had never said so much as a single word.

"The thing is, my own room and my own bed and my own friends are comfy and cozy and... mine. Everything here is new."

"That doesn't make any sense at all," Zoomi said, shaking her head. "We belong to each other. You've known me since you were a tiny baby carrying toy-me around everywhere, and I've been waiting for you to arrive for probably at least three thousand years."

"You do look like my old Zoomi. But you're a new Zoomi," Zoe said carefully. "New can be nice. I like new shoes! And new crayons before they break. And new backpacks at the beginning of the school year."

"And new moon letters in the alphaberry pie?" Zoomi asked.

"Probably?" Zoe said.

"And new friends?" Zoomi asked.

"I think so," Zoe said.

Zoomi scooted a little closer to Zoe. "Me too," she said.

Then Zoe did something new. She held Zoomi's fuzzy, friendly, enormous hand. It was so soft and so warm.

"Moo's hand was a lot louder than yours," Zoomi mused.

"Louder?" Zoe asked.

"Yeah. Yours hardly plays any music at all."

"It doesn't play any, actually."

"Oh. Well, it's still a nice hand. Sorry it's not musical."

"That's okay," Zoe said, smiling. "I'd like to know more about musical hands. And moon letters."

"I'd like to know more about backpacks," Zoomi said. "And freckles."

"Maybe we can still be friends, even if I don't stay forever?"

"Maybe," Zoomi said. "Especially if we do a good job on the rainbow mud slide."

"I still don't know what that is," Zoe said.

"I'll show you," Zoomi said, smiling even bigger.

Chapter Nine

Zoomi couldn't wait to show Zoe the slide. Izly and Doug joined them for the walk

around the hill to find the path to the slide, and all three of them watched as Zoe did something absolutely spectacular and completely terrifying with her feet in the air and her hands on the ground. She did three of them in a row, like it was nothing.

But as they walked up, up, up the hill, Zoe had questions.

"So is the rainbow slide slippery? And what happens if I do it wrong, does it hurt? I get dizzy, will it make me dizzy?" Zoe asked. Zoomi wished Zoe would take a breath so that Zoomi could ask how to do the feet in the air trick

and if that would make *Zoomi* dizzy, but Zoe didn't take any breaths at all. "Should I go feetfirst? On my back? Or hands first on my belly? Or some other way? Don't say headfirst on my back, that's the scariest way."

"We put extra rainbow mud on it," Zoomi said, gesturing to the longest, twistiest, turniest, muddiest slide in all of GlumbleGlibble. "So it will be fast. Faster than fast. And we have to hold hands the whole way. No matter what happens. And if we can do that, you'll always be my Happy Helpful Human and I'll always be your Zoomi. Okay?"

Zoe did not look okay.

"I'm scared of heights. Especially on twisty slides," she said. "And I don't like mud very much. It's so . . . squelchy. Isn't there something else we could do together? Like eat more cake?"

"Absolutely not," Zoomi said. "Holding hands while sliding down the rainbow mud slide is very serious. It's the only way to become true friends."

Zoe looked scared. Zoomi was trying to understand. Rainbow mud was definitely squelchy. And twisty slides could make you pretty dizzy. But they were also so fun. "We'll do it together," she told Zoe. "And then when we're done, you can teach me something new and scary. Like that thing you did. With your legs in the air."

"A cartwheel?"

"A cartwheel. Wow. Yes. I can't believe I got the one Human in the world who can do a cartwheel."

"I'm not–"

"If you can cartwheel, this is nothing," Zoomi said. "Do you trust me?"

Zoomi was surprised when Zoe whispered, "Yes."

Chapter Ten

"First, we hold hands!" Zoomi said, putting her furry hand out for Zoe to hold. Zoomi still looked a little disappointed that Zoe's hand didn't make noises.

"Now we slide!" Zoomi said.

"We just—go?"

"Yes. It's mostly like going down a regular slide but also it feels like a roller coaster and playing in the snow. And eating lasagna. It's a little like eating lasagna," Zoomi said.

Zoe didn't know what to make of that. She liked lasagna and snow, but not roller coasters.

"Zoomi, maybe we should—" she started. But Zoomi wasn't waiting.

Instead Zoomi sat right down on the slide and shouted, "Here we goooooo!"

But Zoe didn't go. She wasn't ready. She let go of Zoomi's hand.

Zoomi slid down the slide alone.

"What happened???" Zoomi said when she reached the bottom.

"I said I wasn't ready," Zoe said. "I don't understand it yet."

"I explained it perfectly," Zoomi replied, zooming back up to the top of the rainbow mud slide.

Zoe wanted a list of rules. She wanted a checklist and a coach and a teacher and a whole month to practice. She wished Zoomi could understand. But Zoomi didn't know anything about checklists or practicing. Zoomi just zoomed.

She grabbed Zoe's hand again, and Zoe tried to let go but Zoomi held on hard, and this time Zoe toppled down the whole slide sideways because she was so startled. She screamed.

It didn't feel like playing in the snow or eating lasagna. It felt a little like a roller coaster, or like a thunderstorm. Actually, it felt a little like the first time she tried a cartwheel.

"Zoomi!" Zoe yelled. "I said I needed more time! I need to understand more! I need a checklist!" Her heart was pounding from the twists and speed of the slide.

Zoomi looked genuinely confused. "But I figured you'd understand how it is after you did it," she said.

"I don't know how to explain that I need to know everything before I try something," Zoe said.

"Well, *I* don't know how to explain that you can't know everything *until* you try something," Zoomi said.

"Oh, no," Doug said. Doug and Izly had been watching everything with worried looks. "They're arguing. Happy Helpful Humans don't argue."

"I guess that's it. It's over. You obviously can't be friends if you argue. You can't even be in the same room. Or on the same

slide," Izly said. "It was nice while it lasted. I guess we'll all have to pretend this never happened. And let it ruin everything. What other solution could there be?"

"Um. We could try again?" Zoe asked. "And just, like, talk about it?"

Zoomi, Izly, and Doug looked at Zoe as though she'd asked them to count all the stars in the sky and then multiply that number by all the blades of grass in GlumbleGlibble.

Chapter Eleven

Zoomi and Zoe sat. And talked.

Zoomi had never sat and talked through a problem before. It was sort of nice! And also impossible. And also fun! And also really hard work.

"Can we call this having a topsy-turvy-talkie-try?" Zoomi asked. "It seems like it could be a very important part of a Tricky Turnaround."

"Will that help?" Zoe asked.

"Of course," Zoomi said. Giving something a fun name always helped. Humans really didn't know much of anything, it turned out.

"The thing is," Zoe started, "I don't like mud. Or slides. I like rainbows! But that's really it."

"You like rainbows more than *mud*?" Zoomi asked. She was trying as hard as she could to understand, but nothing her Human said made any sense at all.

"I don't really like to be dirty. Or dizzy," Zoe explained.

Zoomi had no idea what to say. She was almost always dirty. Or dizzy. Or both, ideally. Why did she get a Happy Helpful Human that she had nothing in common with? "How can we become best friends if we don't even like the same things? And if we don't hold hands down the rainbow mud slide?"

"Maybe there's some other way to do it?" Zoe asked.

Zoomi looked to her friends Izly and Doug, who looked just as baffled as she felt.

"Another way?" Izly asked. "Like . . . backward? Or on your tummy?"

"I meant more like, maybe Zoomi can go down by herself and I'll cheer her on. Or maybe we can just do something else? Have a picnic or something?"

"A picnic?" Doug asked. "That sounds awful. Is that like a rash?"

Zoe laughed. "No, it's getting some sandwiches and eating outside on a blanket together. It's nice. It's what me and my best friend Kyla do every weekend. Used to do."

"So you're saying, we could be friends by doing something *else*?" Zoomi asked, trying to make sure she understood. "Or by doing the rainbow mud slide in a different way that doesn't upset you?"

"Exactly!" Zoe said.

Zoomi wanted to go down the slide holding hands. She wanted to have her

Human be like every other Human who came to GlumbleGlibble.

Except.

She also really wanted her Human to be Zoe.

And maybe Zoe could only really be Zoe, the way Zoomi was Zoomi and Izly was Izly and Doug was always Doug.

"Okay," Zoomi said. "Let's try it your way."

She did a somersault and raced down the slide on her back with her legs up in the air. She thought it would feel lonely, but Zoe was at the bottom cheering, singing a little song about how fast Zoomi was going. Izly and Doug followed her, excited to practice for the arrival of their own Happy Helpful Humans.

And when they got to the bottom, there was a picnic of sunbutter and sunbeam sandwiches.

It wasn't like a rash at all.

And it wasn't quite like holding hands down the rainbow mud slide either.

But it was theirs.

Chapter Twelve

Zoe ate three sunbutter and sunbeam sandwiches. She rode on Zoomi's shoulders up and down Happy Helpful Human Hill. She had made a real new friend. Or sort of new. Zoomi was everything Zoe had dreamed she might be when she was carrying stuffie-Zoomi in her backpack to kindergarten. But she was also so much more.

Zoe could hardly believe she had traveled to GlumbleGlibble and been lifted away by balloons and had even stuck one finger into the rainbow mud, just to see what it felt like. It was gooey and sparkly and strange.

Maybe she'd ride it down a slide again someday. Maybe.

"What are we going to do now?" Zoomi asked. She was jumping up and down with excitement. "Do you want to learn the GlumbleGlibble Gallop? Or go to the moon for moonburgers? Oh, or you can finally teach me one of your wheeliecarts?"

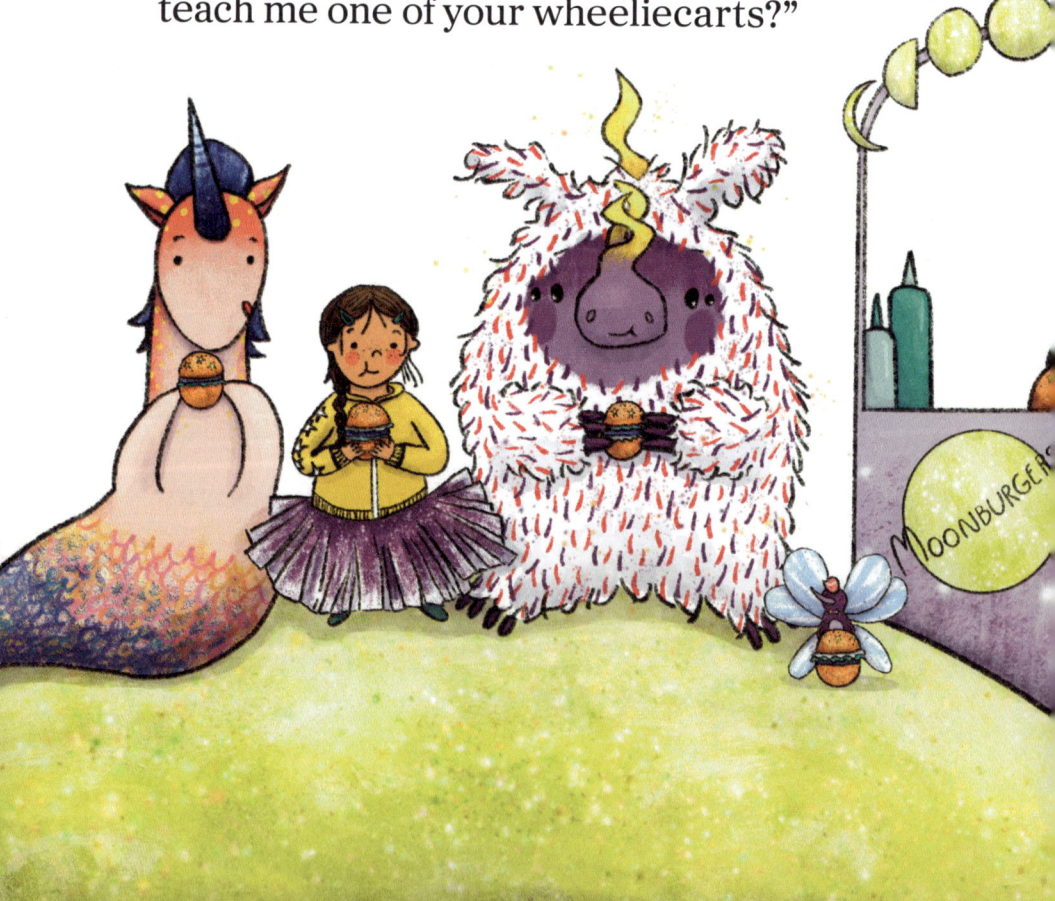

"A cartwheel," Zoe said. "I can teach you a cartwheel. But then, um, I have to go."

Zoomi stopped jumping.

She also stopped smiling.

"Go?"

"Go home," Zoe said as gently as she could.

"I thought you might consider never leaving," Zoomi said. "In GlumbleGlibble we could picnic every day. We can ride unicorns. We can play cloud tag! Don't you want to play cloud tag?"

"That all sounds amazing," Zoe said. "But I live in Sherborn. I can't live here. I can visit, though."

"Every day?" Zoomi asked.

"Most days," Zoe promised. "Unless I have a school concert or something. I'm thinking of picking up the tuba."

Zoomi beamed. "I'd like to see that," she said.

"Maybe someday you can visit Sherborn," Zoe suggested.

"Are there dishwashers there? I've always wanted to see a dishwasher."

"Of course," Zoe said.

"And fire hydrants??"

"Yep."

"And you."

"And me," Zoe said with a smile.

They had almost reached the pineapple portal that Zoe would go through to return to her home. She tried to memorize exactly what it looked like, to be sure she'd know exactly how to get back. She'd already lost Zoomi once, and she was a little scared of losing her again.

"Okay, Zoomi. I'll see you tomorrow?" Zoe said. She waved to Izly and Doug.

Zoomi looked uncertain. "When Moo and I said goodbye at the end of a fun day we would do a special handshake and sing three songs and make an Ice Cream Wednesday and ride our dinosaurs all the way home together."

Zoe was curious what an Ice Cream Wednesday was.

"Maybe next time?" she said.

"But Moo and I—"

"I'm Zoe," Zoe said. "I'm not Moo."

Zoomi was very quiet.

"And you're not Kyla," Zoe said.

Zoomi nodded slowly.

"We're Zoomi and Zoe," Zoe said.

"Zoomi and Zoe, Brave Superheroes of GlumbleGlibble! Zoomi and Zoe, Wheelie-cart Champions! Zoomi and Zoe, Tuba-

Playing Geniuses!" Zoomi said, getting more and more excited with each new Zoomi idea. "Zoomi and Zoe, Conquerors of the Tricky Turnaround!"

"Zoomi and Zoe, new friends," Zoe said.

And Zoomi gave Zoe the biggest hug in all of GlumbleGlibble. There weren't shoe-shaped cakes or mountains of toothpaste or garbage. There wasn't a flurry of glitter or even a single balloon. But it was magical all the same.

COREY ANN HAYDU is the author of many critically acclaimed books for young readers. She lives in Brooklyn with her husband and two young daughters, and you can visit her online at coreyannhaydu.com.

ANNE APPERT is an illustrator and storyteller who uses humor and whimsy to inspire kids to dream big and love themselves. You can visit Anne at anneappert.com.

Don't miss Zoomi and Zoe's second adventure:

Zoomi & Zoe and the sibling situation

Coming August 2025!

David Borgenicht Chairman and Founder
Jhanteigh Kupihea President and Publisher
Nicole De Jackmo EVP, Deputy Publisher
Andie Reid Creative Director
Jane Morley Managing Editor
Mandy Sampson Production Director
Shaquona Crews Principal, Contracts and Rights
Katherine McGuire Assistant Director of Subsidiary Rights

CREATIVE

Alex Arnold Editorial Director, Children's
Jess Zimmerman Editor
Rebecca Gyllenhaal Associate Editor
Jessica Yang Assistant Editor
Elissa Flanigan Senior Designer
Paige Graff Junior Designer
Kassie Andreadis Managing Editorial Assistant

SALES, MARKETING, AND PUBLICITY

Kate Brown Senior Sales Manager
Christina Tatulli Digital Marketing Manager
Ivy Weir Senior Publicity and Marketing Manager
Gaby Iori Publicist and Marketing Coordinator
Kim Ismael Digital Marketing Design Associate
Scott MacLean Publicity and Marketing Assistant
Jesse Mendez Sales Assistant

OPERATIONS

Kaitlyn Buszkiewic Finance Manager
Caprianna Anderson Business Associate
Robin Wright Production and Sales Assistant